Me Throw
the B

By **Mo Willems**
An **ELEPHANT & PIGGIE** Book
Hyperion Books for Children/*New York*

AN IMPRINT OF DISNEY BOOK GROUP

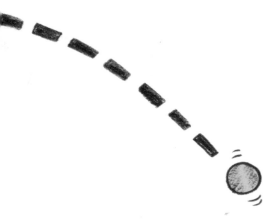

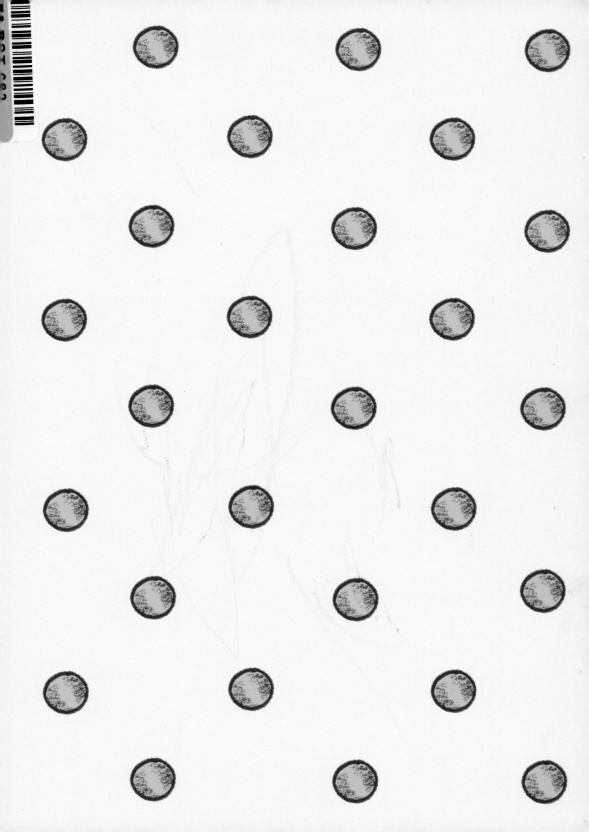

For Max, Sam, Amanda, and Irving

Text and illustrations copyright © 2009 by Mo Willems

Printed in Singapore
Reinforced binding

First Edition, March 2009
10
F850-6835-5-15087

Library of Congress Cataloging-in-Publication Data on file.
ISBN 978-1-4231-1348-5

Visit www.hyperionbooksforchildren.com and www.pigeonpresents.com

La, la, la!

This is
your ball?

8

9

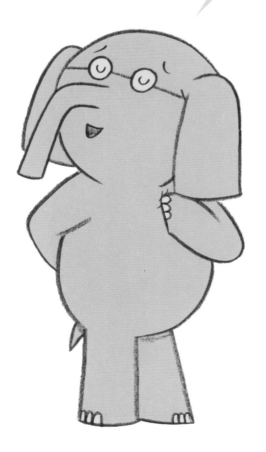

I am very good
at throwing.

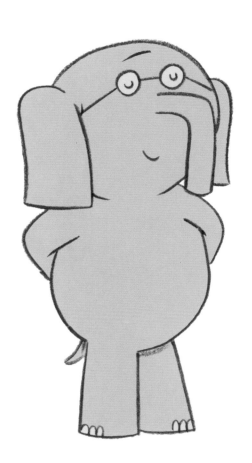

I worked very hard to learn how to throw a ball.

23

THE PIG IS

FLING!

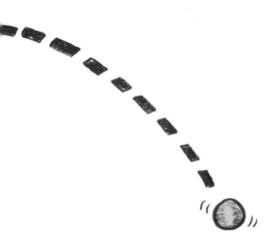

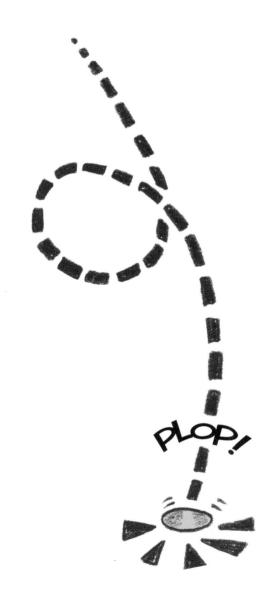

PLOP!

35

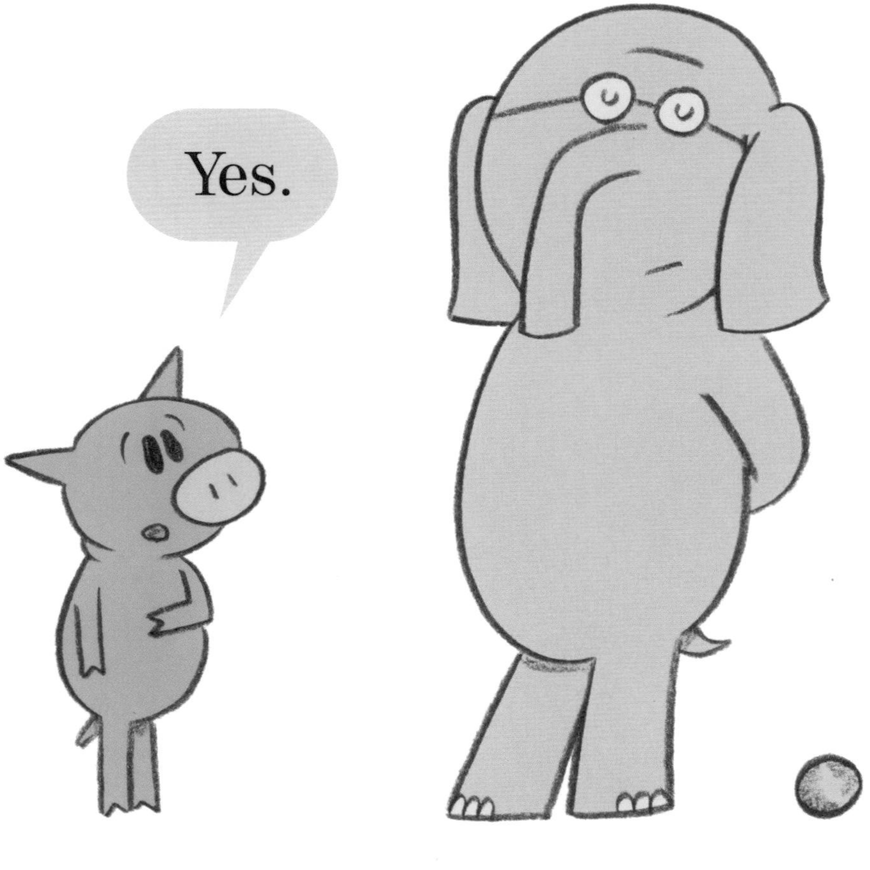
Yes.

43

But I
had fun!

FLING!

56

Elephant and Piggie have more funny adventures in:

Today I Will Fly!

My Friend Is Sad

I Am Invited to a Party!

There Is a Bird on Your Head!
(Theodor Seuss Geisel Medal)

I Love My New Toy!

I Will Surprise My Friend!

Are You Ready to Play Outside?
(Theodor Seuss Geisel Medal)

Elephants Cannot Dance!

Pigs Make Me Sneeze!

I Am Going!

Can I Play Too?

We Are in a Book!
(Theodor Seuss Geisel Honor)

I Broke My Trunk!
(Theodor Seuss Geisel Honor)

Should I Share My Ice Cream?

Happy Pig Day!

Listen to My Trumpet!

Let's Go for a Drive!
(Theodor Seuss Geisel Honor)

A Big Guy Took My Ball!
(Theodor Seuss Geisel Honor)

I'm a Frog!

My New Friend Is So Fun!

Waiting Is Not Easy!
(Theodor Seuss Geisel Honor)